Crystal Shards
Short stories from the Crystal Tower
Volume 1
Judy Lunsford

Table of Contents

Crystal Shards
Short stories from the Crystal Tower
Volume 1
Judy Lunsford

Included in this collection:
Introduction from the author
Rumtuskin of the Emberdiggers
Seeking Garille
The Indigo-Eyed Pup

Introduction

This is a short collection of stories from my Crystal Tower epic fantasy series. It is a quick introduction to some of my favorite characters the appear throughout the series.

The title characters are the ones that are my favorites, although the whole crew in Rumtuskin of the Emberdiggers, as well as Shyeanna in Seeking Garille fit into my favorite characters category as well.

I hope you enjoy this sneak peek into the series. All of the stories can stand alone, so if you haven't had the chance to read the series, this is a great introduction to some of the characters you will meet along the way.

Happy Reading!

Judy Lunsford

March 2022

RUMTUSKIN OF THE EMBERDIGGERS

The purple velvet tree was highly sought after by magicians and sorcerers everywhere. This made life complicated for them. Burble was no exception.

His beautifully hued leaves were the softest foliage available. Softer than any fabric made by human hands. They had a faint scent of the forest to them, one which could never be overpowered by any other odor.

His leaves were also very susceptible to magic. Burble's delicate leaves were perfect for spells, potions, and charms. But the best magic was tailor magic.

Clothing made from the leaves of the purple velvet tree were seamless and durable and the most comfortable cloth. They did not rip or tear easily, and were almost strong enough to be a light layer of armor.

Burble had many brushes with velvet hunters. He was defenseless, for the most part. He moved rather slowly, usually tripping himself on his own roots, which were shallow enough that he could move across the ground with fair, if slow, ease.

The main defense of the purple velvet trees were their symbiotes. A long vine of ivy wrapped itself around the trunk of every velvet tree. But it wasn't any common ivy. It was a crawling attack ivy.

Burble's symbiote was named Crawl. But the symbiote did more than crawl. He was faster than lightning, and he had no qualms about strangling any hunter that came too close to Burble. The ivy was also stronger than iron chains, almost impossible to break without a tremendous amount of strength.

The symbiote ivy lived off of the sap produced by the purple velvet tree. It was their only source of food. And the sap was toxic to the purple velvet tree. Without a crawling ivy, the purple velvet trees would die. Without a tree, the ivy would die. So, Crawl had good reason to protect Burble with his life.

Crawl had been with Burble for as long as he could remember. Crawling ivy finds young velvet trees almost instinctively. And they are joined for life. They both have exceptionally long lifespans, so they have centuries together.

Burble was unique, even among the other purple velvet trees. He had allergies. And the thing he was most allergic to was himself. Or he thought he was. Burble was also a hypochondriac.

Burble would sneeze if his leaves came too close to his trunk. Usually with drooping leaves like a weeping willow, velvet trees had long flowing wispy branches that fell down around them gracefully like a veil. But Burble kept his branches held away from himself, lest the velvet brush against his bark in a place where Crawl did not serve as protection.

Burble was a rather young tree. He was looking forward to his eighty-fifth spring. He and Crawl always celebrated by going to a special lake in the middle of the forest, where they were joined for the first time. It was a breeding ground for the purple velvet trees in the fall, but in mid-spring, it was usually frequented by the younger trees who still bothered to celebrate their birthday.

It was eerily quiet when they got there. Burble slowed his approach to the lake. The air was filled with the scent of the grass of the meadow, but not of any other velvet trees.

There were usually at least a few other velvet trees scattered around. It was a beautiful waterhole, surrounded by a small meadow where the velvet trees had an easy time moving around. The sounds of spring were normal, with birds singing, and small rabbits hopping here and there. Rabbits were particularly fond of velvet trees, and the meadow was usually full of them, with the baby rabbits hopping through the meadow to greet the velvet trees as they arrived.

But there were no birds singing, and the meadow was empty of rabbits. Not a single one was to be seen.

"Where is everyone?" Burble asked.

"Get back into the woods," Crawl ordered. "Something is very wrong."

Burble started to move back towards the cover of the woods, but before he could get very far, it was already too late. An owlephant came lumbering through the meadow from a not far away.

Although rare in this part of the forest, owlephants did wander to the lake occasionally. The beast had the body and trunk of an elephant, but the head and wings of an owl. The talons on their bulbous feet were sharp enough to strip leaves and bark in a single swipe. An adult owlephant could knock over a velvet tree and pin them to the ground, rendering the tree helpless while made into a meal.

Burble stared in horror at the beast. Owlephants loved the leaves of the velvet trees. It was their favorite tasty snack. It caught sight of Burble and started to charge.

"Move," Crawl demanded. "I can't take it on myself. It's too big."

Burble started to move, but he wasn't fast enough. The huge beast caught up to them in seconds and Burble was nowhere near close enough to the trees to be able to escape from the owlephant.

It reached its trunk out to grab Burble by some branches as Crawl shot out and wrapped himself around the neck of the beast.

The owlephant reared back in shock and let out an ear-piercing roar. Crawl tried to tighten around the thick leathery skin where it met the feathers leading up to the creature's head. It was the only sweet spot that Crawl had to defeat the creature on his own.

Burble shrieked in horror and tried to pull away from the beast.

"Don't pull," Crawl demanded. "You're stretching me too much."

The elephant tried to lean away from Crawl, hoping to break his vine. Crawl held on around the beast's neck, but didn't have the traction he needed to hold him. The owlephant reared back and Crawl lost his grip, giving the beast a chance to catch its breath.

But while the creature was still reared up, a dwarf came from out of nowhere. He hefted his spear and rammed it through the side of the soft flesh under the owlephant's armpit, where the feathers of the wing met the leathery skin, and drove it sideways into the beast's heart.

The owlephant made the worst noise Burble had ever heard, shaking leaves from the trees above them, and then fell backwards with an earth quaking thud. It moved its legs a little, as reflexes tried to simulate escape, and then the beast lay quiet, the life gone from it forever.

The dwarf knelt by the beast's side. He removed his red hat and placed it over his heart as he bid the beast farewell. Dwarves took death very seriously, and tried to never let their victims die alone. The only exception was in times of war, where there was no time for the dead.

Crawl tried to disentangle himself from around the beast's neck, but he was pinned to the ground on the underside.

When the dwarf was finished, he noticed Crawl trying to quietly escape while Burble tried to tilt the beast off of his symbiote. The dwarf went and found a large stick and wedged it under the beast and used it as leverage to help the ivy free himself.

"Thank you for your assistance," Crawl said, once disentangled and once again wrapped safely around Burble's trunk.

"My pleasure," the dwarf said.

"We would offer you a reward for your bravery, but alas, we have nothing," Burble said politely.

"On the contrary," the dwarf said. "You have much that I need."

"You're a hunter?" Crawl bristled and was ready to attack again. "But dwarves have little interest in velvet trees."

"I am not a hunter," the dwarf said. "I am Rumtuskin of the Emberdiggers. I am a humble tailor."

The dwarf took off his hat and bowed deeply to Burble and Crawl. He straightened and smiled as he put his hat back into place.

"My name is Burble, and my ivy is Crawl," Burble said. "We are very grateful for your assistance. But we can't allow you to strip my leaves."

"I have no desire to strip your leaves," Rumtuskin said. "As I said, I am not a hunter."

"Then what do you want,' Crawl growled.

"I've been watching the two of you for some time," Rumtuskin said. "I have noticed that Burble tends to sneeze off his own leaves on a fairly regular basis."

"You've been following us?" Burble was amazed.

"How have I not sensed your presence?" Crawl demanded.

"I have stayed at a safe distance," Rumtuskin said. "I follow you far behind, and I collect the stray leaves from the ground."

Rumtuskin reached into a red leather pouch at his belt. He pulled out a piece of cloth, velvety and purple, obviously made from the leaves of velvet trees. It was seamless and beautiful.

"Oh, pretty," Burble cooed. "Is that made from me?"

"Yes," Rumtuskin smiled proudly. "If you would still like to offer a reward for my assistance, all I ask is that you allow me to travel with you. I will only pick up what falls naturally. But I will no longer have to chase the leaves in the breeze."

"Sure," Burble said cheerfully.

"No," Crawl said at the same time.

"Why not?" Burble asked.

"I don't trust him," Crawl said.

"But he saved us from the owlephant," Burble said. "And he was following us anyway."

"That's the part I don't like," Crawl said. "How do we know he isn't out to assassinate the King?"

"The King?" Rumtuskin asked. "Which King?"

"King DaeMark, of the Crystal Tower," Burble said.

"Don't tell him which King," Crawl tried to stop Burble but was too late.

"I can assure you that I am not an assassin," Rumtuskin said. "And if you are on your way to pay respects to the King, I will gladly wait behind at an encampment while you are there."

"You can come with us to meet the King," Burble said.

"No, he will wait for us," Crawl corrected. "The dwarves and the humans don't get along."

"King DaeMark gets along with everyone," Burble said.

"So that means I can come along with you?" Rumtuskin asked.

"For now," Crawl said. "But one wrong move and I will strangle you while you sleep."

"Agreed," Rumtuskin said happily.

Burble relaxed for the first time since he saw the owlephant and his branches accidentally brushed against his bark. He let out a loud sneeze and leaves rained down around them.

"Excuse me," Rumtuskin said. "That's my cue."

The dwarf scurried around and picked up every last leaf and tucked them gently into his leather pouch.

"If you'd like, I can show you how I magic them together when we stop for the night," Rumtuskin said.

"Oh, I would like that very much," Burble squealed. "Very much indeed."

WHEN THE THREE REACHED a suitable campsite for the night, they stopped and started to make camp.

Burble and Crawl were used to just finding a place where Burble had enough space to rest for the night. But having a dwarf travelling with them made stopping for the night a little more complicated.

After passing three sites that Crawl thought were perfectly suitable, they finally found a place with a small clearing near a stream. Burble was happy to have water nearby and soaked his roots thoroughly.

They were surrounded securely by a nice assortment of trees and bushes, and the soft ground was covered with a nutritious moss for Burble.

Rumtuskin stopped and looked around the area and drew in a deep breath.

"Ah," he said. "I love the smell of the river moss. It reminds me of when I left the mountains with my mother to go gathering."

"You went gathering with your mother?" Crawl said. "I thought the dwarves lived within the mountains."

"We do," Rumtuskin said. "But my mother was half gnome. So she liked to venture out of the mountain and into the woods. It made her feel more at home. The smells of the trees and flowers, the sounds of the birds. The feel of wet earth under her feet. The smell of rain. She needed all of that once in a while. Eventually, I did too."

"What did she gather?" Burble asked.

"Herbs, roots, and plants mostly," Rumtuskin said. "She was a healer, so she needed to replenish her supplies."

Crawl kept his eyes on Rumtuskin as he went about making camp.

Rumtuskin found a nice flat piece of ground near the base of some trees. He started to pull things out of his red leather pouch. A bedroll, a small tarp, and a pillow, all made from what appeared to be velvet leaves.

He made a small sleeping space and then moved on to an open area and proceeded to make a campfire. Once the fire was lit, he pulled a little cooking pot and some rations out of his pouch.

Crawl couldn't take it any longer, "How does all of that fit into that tiny little hip pouch?"

Rumtuskin looked up at Crawl and smiled, "It's a magic pouch. It will hold just about anything I put in it."

"What won't it hold?" Burble asked.

"What do you mean?" Rumtuskin asked.

"You said it will hold just about anything you put in it," Burble said. "What won't it hold?"

Rumtuskin looked down at the little pouch. "I actually don't know. I've never had anything that didn't fit into it. But I haven't really tried to put anything that remarkable into it."

"What is it made out of?" Crawl asked. "Everything else you have seems to be made from Burble's leaves."

"It was made by my mother," Rumtuskin said. "It's the pouch she used to gather her herbs in. The magic she used is magic that I am not talented in, but my father gave it to me after my mother died."

"Oh, I'm sorry about your mother," Burble said. "Has it been long?"

Rumtuskin suddenly looked very sad and shook his head. "It's been less than a year."

"Oh, I'm so sorry, Rumtuskin," Burble said. "Is that why you're gathering?"

Rumtuskin nodded. "My mother always said I should develop my magic. Tailor magic is a rare skill among the dwarves. Even among the gnomes. But I never was brave enough to pursue it."

"What did your father say about it?" Crawl asked.

"He was always against it," Rumtuskin said. "Until my mother died. Then he suddenly said I should follow my heart."

"What changed his mind?" Burble asked.

"My mother," Rumtuskin said. "My father took a lot of abuse from other dwarves about marrying my mother. But he followed his heart. When she died, he said he would never have chosen differently. It was then that he realized that I needed to follow my heart too. He gave me her gathering bag and told me to pursue learning my tailor magic. He gave me his blessing and sent me on my way."

"Wow," Burble said. "Is that when you found us.?"

"No," Rumtuskin shook his head. "I found another tailor magician in a village. He took me on as an apprentice, but after a few months, he had taught me all he knew."

"A few months?" Crawl said.

"Yes," Rumtuskin said. "He wasn't very good. But he was very nice. He taught me some basics and helped me get through some of my grief. And his wife was a wonderful cook."

Rumtuskin sat down in front of the fire and started putting his dinner together. He put his rations into the little pot and hung it over the fire with a stick and a hook.

"I would offer you both some, but I don't think we eat the same things," Rumtuskin said.

"The moss on the ground is plenty for me, but thank you," Burble said. "And Crawl is taken care of."

"I've read a lot about your kind," Rumtuskin said. "But you two were the first I had come across. And when I realized that Burble shed his leaves naturally, I just started following you."

"That's quite all right," Burble said. "You've been wonderful company. The only one I have to talk to is Crawl, and he's a grump."

"Hey," Crawl objected.

"Well, you are," Burble said.

"Well, I thank you for allowing me to accompany you," Rumtuskin said. "And I will gladly show you any of my tailor magics if you would like to watch."

"I still don't trust him," Crawl whispered.

"As for your King," Rumtuskin said. "I mean him no harm. And I will wait wherever you would like me to when you visit him."

"I think you should come with us," Burble said.

"What?" Crawl and Rumtuskin said in unison.

"I think you would be a wonderful liaison for the dwarves," Burble said. "King DaeMark is a kind man. Maybe you can help establish peace between your people and his."

"I can't speak for my people," Rumtuskin said. "They would never allow it."

"Well, then," Burble said. "You will come as our guest."

"We can't do that," Crawl whispered.

"Yes, we can," Burble said. "And we are."

"I accept your offer on one condition," Rumtuskin said. "If the King does not wish to have me there, I leave. I don't want to cause trouble."

"Agreed," Burble said. "But I guarantee you that the King will be happy to greet you as an honored guest."

"We'll see," Crawl grumbled.

SOMETIME, LONG AFTER midnight, there was a rustling in the trees above the small camp. The fire was still burning, and it cast a soft glow across the sleeping figures and disappeared into the darkness.

Crawl awoke first and stared up into the shadowy branches of the trees against the night sky.

"Alert," Crawl yelled. "Alert! Wake up!"

Burble woke up quickly and Rumtuskin was already on his feet.

"What's the matter?" Rumtuskin asked.

"Drop bears!" Crawl said. "Be ready."

Rumtuskin pulled a small sword out of his pouch and waited for the inevitable attack. "Drop bears?"

"They hunt in small packs," Crawl warned.

"What do they eat?' Rumtuskin asked.

"Anything they can find," Burble answered.

Moments later, the first small fuzzy creature fell from the treetops. It was followed by a small shower of several more.

Burble used his branches to swat them away while Crawl and Rumtuskin put up a fight. After a short flurry of Crawl catching the leaping bears, Rumtuskin ran them through.

When the short battle was over, Rumtuskin squatted down next to one of the creatures and looked at it.

"They're really kind of cute," Rumtuskin said.

"I know," Burble said. "It's a shame to have to fight them."

"They eat dwarves as well as tree bark," Crawl reminded them.

Rumtuskin looked around at the small mass of fluffy bears. There were about a half dozen of them laying around their encampment. "Now what?"

"Your pouch," Burble cried.

Rumtuskin turned in the direction that Burble was stretching his branches.

Rumtuskin's pouch had been kicked to the side in the scuffle with the bears and had landed at the edge of the fire. One side of it was already ablaze.

"No," Rumtuskin raced towards the fire and pulled the pouch to safety and stomped the fire out. He stood over it and watched with tears in his eyes as the contents spilled out all over the ground in front of him. His camping supplies, his clothes, and his velvet cloth all laid on the ground next to the smouldering pouch.

"Is it all right?" Burble asked as he made his way over to Rumtuskin's side.

"No," the dwarf shook his head. "The magic is gone. It's just a pouch."

"Can you fix it?" Burble asked.

"No," Rumtuskin shook his head. "I don't know that kind of magic."

"I'm sorry," Burble said. "Can we help?"

Rumtuskin shook his head again, "I just need a moment."

"With the drop bears?" Burble asked.

"No," Rumtuskin shook his head. "Not with the drop bears."

Burble and Crawl gave Rumtuskin a few minutes alone. He sat by the fire with his mother's pouch and stared at the red leather. He ran his fingers over the runes that had been engraved in it by his mother's hands and then held it close to his chest.

After a few minutes, Crawl spoke up.

"I don't mean to rush you," Crawl said. "But scavengers will be along soon for the bears."

"It will be dawn soon," Rumtuskin agreed. "We should move."

Rumtuskin collected his things and made a small backpack out of his bedroll and some rope that he had stashed with his gear. When all of his things were collected and tucked safely away, he hoisted the pack onto his shoulders and kicked out the fire.

"We should go," Rumtuskin said quietly.

RUMTUSKIN REMAINED quiet for most of the journey. They finally hit the paths leading to the city of Shal Tahl. Burble moved slowly along the gravel, so progress was slow as they headed towards the Crystal Tower where the King lived.

"Over this hill, there is a large meadow, we can pick up speed there," Crawl said to Rumtuskin.

The dwarf nodded.

As they reached the peak of the hill, they stopped and stared at what they saw.

The town was being raided by soldiers, and there was chaos everywhere. People were running through the streets being chased by the enemy soldiers. Homes burned from fires set by the general's torches.

"What's happening?" Rumtuskin asked.

"Those soldiers are from Talask's army," Burble said.

"Who's?" Rumtuskin asked.

"The King's older brother," Crawl said. "He thinks the kingdom is rightfully his, but their father disowned him."

"For what?" Rumtuskin asked.

"For things like this," Burble said.

The King's army was filling the village. They started to battle Talask's soldiers.

"There's the King," Burble said.

"Where?" Rumtuskin was having trouble finding him in the crowd.

"There," Burble said. "With the family with the baby."

Rumtuskin looked and saw the King pulling a young couple out of harm's way. He pushed them in the direction of safety, and then turned to fight one of Talask's men.

The young man drew his sword and fought by the King's side.

His wife hesitated for a moment, and then hid the baby among a pile of baskets in front of a small shop. She then took a sword from a fallen man nearby and fought alongside her husband.

"We have to help," Rumtuskin said. "Look!"

Rumtuskin dropped his backpack and took off running through the meadow.

Burble and Crawl saw what the dwarf was pointing at.

One of the generals was heading through the town setting shops on fire and the basket shop was in his path.

Rumtuskin ran as fast as his legs could carry him and he made it to the basket shop in time to grab the basket that the baby was in. The general started to set fire to the basket stand and saw Rumtuskin with the child.

"Just where do you think you're going with a human child?" the general looked down at Rumtuskin and the baby.

Rumtuskin didn't say anything, he just picked up the basket with the child in it and adjusted her blanket. Her sweet face looked up at him as he covered her mouth and nose and tucked the pale pink fabric in around her face. He ignored the smoke in the air that was starting to choke him. He carefully put the basket over one shoulder and turned to run.

"That baby is mine," the general said. "Give it to me."

The general started after Rumtuskin but was stopped by the King's voice behind him.

"Talask!"

Rumtuskin stared wide eyed back at the general, who stopped and turned to look at the King.

"Little brother," he tossed the torch into the last of the baskets and pulled out his sword. "I've been waiting for this moment."

Rumtuskin seized the moment to take the baby and run.

RUMTUSKIN KEPT HIS eyes focused on the path towards the top of the hill. He tried not to jiggle the baby too much, but to no avail. She lay in the basket and cried as he ran with her in the basket back towards Burble and Crawl. His lungs burned with the effort and the sting of the smoke, but he made it to the top and laid the basket down under the safety of Burble's branches.

Rumtuskin checked on the baby, and cooed to her softly to get her to stop crying. He scurried to his pack and pulled out a small rag, his water bag, and his sword.

"What are you going to do?" Crawl asked.

Rumtuskin quickly soaked the rag and gave the baby some water. He wiped her face with the cool rag and then picked up his sword.

"Take care of her," Rumtuskin said.

"What?" Crawl asked. "We're not babysitters."

"We will protect her with our lives," Burble said. "For the King."

Rumtuskin took off running down the hill again. He headed back towards the basket shop, in hopes of finding the baby's mother.

He saw her in the distance, battling with one of Talask's men. She was impressive with a sword, and was holding her own quite well. But a second soldier spotted them and went over to join the fight.

Rumtuskin charged at the second soldier, with his small sword held out in front of him. He had never done battle with humans before, but he reminded himself that he had slain an owlephant in the forest, so he charged on. He didn't realize that he was screaming until the soldier turned.

He caught the soldier somewhat by surprise and as he swung around to see who was noisily attacking, Rumtuskin had time to hamstring him, his dwarven blade sharp enough to cut through the soldier's boots.

The man fell to the ground, screaming and Rumtuskin finished him.

He turned to the soldier who was battling with the baby's mother. It was too late. He watched as the baby's mother fell to the ground after the soldier removed his blade from her chest.

Before the soldier could turn around, Rumtuskin did the same attack on him as he had done on his friend. He pushed past the body of the soldier and ran to the baby's mother, who was laying on the ground, gasping for air.

"My baby," she whispered to him. "You have to find my baby."

"I did," Rumtuskin said to her. "She's safe."

The woman smiled weakly. "Thank you."

"Where is your husband?" he asked, looking around for the man who had been fighting at the King's side.

"He's dead," she shook her head. "He defended the King. He was so brave. The King is still alive because of him."

She looked proud for a moment.

"You have to take care of my daughter," she said. "Find her a home. We have no other family."

"I promise," Rumtuskin said.

He held her hand as she gasped for air.

"Her name is Shyeanna," she said. "Please, take care of her."

"I promise, it will be done," Rumtuskin said. "She will be safe."

The woman took her last gasping breath and closed her eyes.

For the first time on a battlefield, Rumtuskin knelt and took off his hat. He took the Dwarvish Time for the Dead in the middle of battle.

TALASK HAD BELIEVED that his brother's soldiers were not in the city that day. He was wrong. It was a hard but short battle. Talask had underestimated the number of soldiers that would come to the town's aid during the attack.

Outnumbered by too large of a ratio, Talask had ordered his remaining soldiers to retreat. Once again, Talask suffered a loss at the hands of his younger brother. Which all but guaranteed that he would be back to fight for what he felt was rightfully his.

King DaeMark helped the townspeople put out the fires and directed the injured be taken to the Crystal Tower's infirmary.

Rumtuskin watched with awe as the King assisted his people. He was one of them, and they accepted him as one of them. There were very few formalities, and he seemed to know a lot of the townspeople by name.

DaeMark finished helping an injured man onto a stretcher and watched as two of his soldiers carried him off to the castle.

The King turned and saw Rumtuskin standing in the middle of the road, his Dwarven sword at his side.

DaeMark approached the dwarf.

"You fought bravely," DaeMark said. "Thank you."

"I was only trying to find the parents of the infant," Rumtuskin said.

"You know where she is?" DaeMark said. "Please, tell me."

"She's at the top of the hill leading into the town to the north," Rumtuskin said. "She's being watched over by some friends."

"Is she all right?" DaeMark asked.

"She's fine," Rumtuskin said. "I promised her mother I would find her a good home."

"She will stay with me," DaeMark said. "Her parents both died in battle by my side, defending me from my brother and his soldiers. She will be my daughter."

Rumtuskin stared at the King.

"Well, then," he gathered himself. "Let me go introduce you to your daughter."

Rumtuskin led the King towards the hill, but Burble and Crawl were already heading down, the basket snuggled up tightly to Burble's trunk by a cooing Crawl.

"Burble, is that you?" DaeMark asked, jogging towards the velvet tree.

"Yes, my King," Burble said. "We kept the baby safe for our friend, Rumtuskin."

DaeMark took the basket from Burble and stared down at the sleeping child.

"The three of you saved her life," DaeMark said. "I thank you."

"Her name is Shyeanna," Rumtuskin said.

DaeMark picked Shyeanna up out of the basket and held her in his arms.

"Hello, beautiful girl," he whispered. "When you wake up, you will be a princess."

THE DAY AFTER THE WOUNDED were tended to, and accommodations were found for those who had lost homes, DaeMark asked Burble, Crawl, and Rumtuskin to meet with him in the Crystal Tower.

They met with him in the conservatory, which was where Burble and Crawl spent a lot of their time while in the city. Burble loved to soak his roots in the spring water that flowed from underground into the indoor greenhouse.

Rumtuskin looked around at the huge glass covered room. There was every kind of plant he could imagine. The scent of the variety of flowers was intoxicating. He had never really smelled flowers growing indoors before. The scents were trapped in the room and magnified by the sun. It was powerful.

"Welcome, my friends," King DaeMark said as he entered the room.

"Your Majesty," Rumtuskin bowed to the King.

"No need for that," DaeMark said. "I don't dwell on formalities. Especially with my friends."

"I'm a friend?" Rumtuskin was amazed. "I barely even know you. And I am a dwarf."

"I know your character," DaeMark said. "I saw you in battle. You are a man of honor. And even more than that, you have a good heart. That is all that matters to me."

"He saw the baby in jeopardy, and he ran down the hill and into battle with no thought for himself," Burble said proudly. "I am honored to call Rumtuskin my friend."

"I am as well," the King said.

"I would like to offer the new princess a gift," Rumtuskin said.

He pulled a baby blanket out of his pack that was made from Burble's leaves. Rumtuskin had worked on it all night. He handed it to the King.

DaeMark ran the fabric through his fingers. "It's absolutely beautiful. I've never seen its equal."

"Thank you," Rumtuskin said.

"He made it from my leaves," Burble said proudly.

"Well, Burble," the King smiled. "You do make the most beautiful leaves of all of your kind."

Crawl stifled a small laugh.

"Thank you for the gift, Rumtuskin," DaeMark said. "The princess will love it."

Rumtuskin nodded and smiled.

"I owe the three of you a debt of gratitude," DaeMark said. "What can I do for you?"

"Nothing," Rumtuskin said. "I do not do battle with honor for a reward."

"I know what you can do," Burble said.

"Name it, old friend," DaeMark said. "And it's yours."

"Would you summon Cassandra here please?" Burble asked.

DaeMark gave Burble an inquisitive look, but asked his guards at the door to do so.

A few minutes later, a gnomish woman entered the room. She was only slightly taller than Rumtuskin and wore a white apron over her pale blue dress. Her dark green hair was pulled into a braid that flowed down her back.

Her hair reminded Rumtuskin of his mother.

Rumtuskin brightened when he saw her and looked between Burble and Cassandra with interest.

"Here she is," DaeMark said. "What do you wish to ask her?"

Burble moved forward to greet the woman. "I don't know if you can help, but my friend Rumtuskin has a bag that was created by his mother. She was half gnome and I was wondering if you knew a similar magic, so you could fix it?"

Rumtuskin gasped and looked at Cassandra.

"What kind of gnomish magic?" she asked.

Crawl produced the pouch and handed it out to Cassandra.

"Where did you get that?" Rumtuskin asked.

"You sleep soundly, my friend," Crawl said.

Cassandra looked it over. She held it in her hands and shut her eyes.

"Oh yes," she said. "I can feel the magic. I know it."

"You can fix it?" Rumtuskin was hopeful.

"I think so, give me a moment," she said.

Cassandra took the pouch over to the spring that Burble had been soaking in and submerged it into the clear spring water.

Rumtuskin gasped as he watched the water completely cover the red leather.

"It will be fine," she said. "Come and watch if you wish."

Rumtuskin and DaeMark both went over and watched over the girl's shoulder.

She sang softly in gnomish to the pouch, weaving her magic into the water.

The burned area on the pouch slowly restored itself, and the pouch started to glow. Her singing increased in rhythm and cadence slightly and she pulled the pouch out of the water.

Rumtuskin hadn't realized that he was holding his breath until he was watching her dry the pouch off with her apron.

She looked up and smiled at Rumtuskin and held the pouch out to him.

"It should be as good as new," she said.

"Thank you," Rumtuskin said.

He reached out to take the bag from her and they both stood there, their eyes locked, each holding the pouch for a moment.

"Your mother's magic was strong," she smiled. "I was able to keep what remained of her magic in it."

"My mother's magic is still there?" Rumtuskin finally took the pouch from her and ran his hand over it once again. This time it was whole and unblemished.

Cassandra nodded. "I used what was left of her magic and weaved in my own."

"Thank you," Rumtuskin said. "How can I ever repay you?"

Cassandra smiled, "Maybe I could make you dinner sometime?"

Rumtuskin blushed. "How would that be me repaying you?"

"I'm sure you'll think of something," Cassandra winked and turned to leave the room.

"Thank you, Cassie," DaeMark grinned as she walked past him.

Rumtuskin watched the girl go in awe.

"She's amazing," Rumtuskin whispered.

Crawl knocked Rumtuskin in the back of his hat.

"I'm sorry," Rumtuskin said, blushing.

"It's not a problem," DaeMark smiled. "She's a wonderful girl, you couldn't find better."

Rumtuskin ran his hands over his pouch once again. "I can't believe it's fixed."

His eyes welled with tears. "I will have to make her something amazing."

"I feel a cold coming on," Burble said. "You'll have your supplies in no time."

"I have one last favor to ask of the three of you," DaeMark said.

"Anything, old friend," Crawl answered.

"I've never raised a child," DaeMark said. "And I think it is only appropriate to ask the ones who rescued her to become her godparents."

Rumtuskin looked at the King in amazement.

"Yes, we would love to," Burble squealed.

"What?" said Crawl.

"You want a dwarf to be the godparent of a princess of Shal Tahl?" Rumtuskin whispered.

"I would love to have such a brave man as an example for my daughter," DaeMark said.

"I would," Rumtuskin stammered. "Yes, I accept."

"That leaves you, Crawl," DaeMark looked at the ivy.

"She's a beautiful child," Crawl said. "I don't know what a symbiote ivy would do for her upbringing, but I humbly accept."

"Then it's settled," DaeMark said. "Rumtuskin, if you would do us the honor of staying with us here in the Crystal Tower, I will have a room set up for you. Just tell me what you need."

"Just a bed and a chair, sir," Rumtuskin said. "I need a place to sleep and to continue to learn my magic."

"I'm sure we can do better than that," DaeMark said. "And don't call me sir. You are my child's godfather, DaeMark will do."

"Yes, sir," Rumtuskin said. "I mean DaeMark."

"You are still learning your tailor magic?" DaeMark asked.

"Yes," Rumtuskin nodded. "I had a teacher, but he didn't know more than basics."

"We have a wonderful tailor here in the Tower," DaeMark said. "And if I'm not mistaken, he's been talking about retiring if he could find an apprentice."

"You mean?" Rumtuskin stammered. "He's here in the castle?"

DaeMark nodded. "I could speak to him for you."

"Yes, please," Rumtuskin nodded happily. "This is all like a dream."

DaeMark laughed. "Not quite. And we must always be ready for Talask's return. Part of the royal tailor's duties is also helping with my soldier's armor."

"That won't be a problem," Rumtuskin said. "I would love to learn whatever he has to teach."

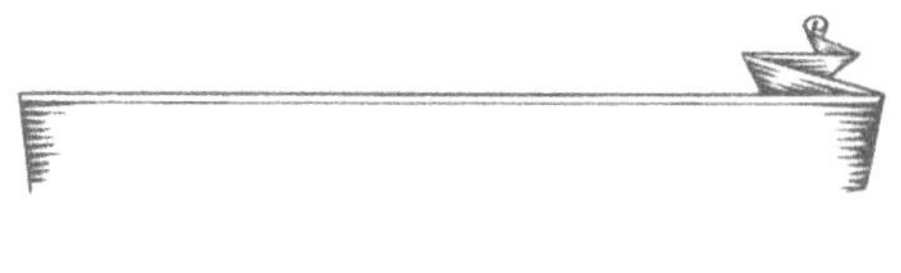

SEEKING GARILLE

Shyeanna traveled for days until she got to the cave where Garille had secluded himself for the last few years.

It was deep in the darkest part of the forest, far from the other dragons.

His shame ran deep. He was the first dragon who had ever failed at his task. The bond had broken. Shattered like glass with a crash that was heard throughout the kingdom and deep into the forests and deserts and even the sea, where all of the dragons trained, hoping one day to be chosen.

Now, because of Garille, hoping that if they are chosen, that they do not fail.

The girl had traveled far, through dangerous terrain. She had to find the red dragon that had hidden himself from all other sentient beings. The one that didn't want to be found.

But she found him nonetheless.

Her mission was to convince the dragon to tell her everything he knew. Everything he could tell her about her uncle. The one who had betrayed the bond with this crushed, but in her mind, still noble beast.

She had left Zalta, her silver dragon, in the woods, preferring to approach by herself. She didn't want the presence of another dragon to damage Garille's spirit any more than it already was.

Another bonded dragon might remind him of his shame, and keep him from giving her the information she so desperately needed.

The entrance of the cave was dark. Shyeanna summoned up her courage and made her way into the blackness. She guided herself through the darkness that engulfed her, sliding her hand against the damp, rocky wall to guide her.

She wished he had a torch. Her footing was unstable as she picked her steps very carefully in the darkness. The dank smell of cold wet dirt felt like it was choking her.

She could see a light far ahead. The flickering light of a fire. She made her way towards it and finally turned a corner to see the red dragon, asleep by the flames that had guided her way. The flickering blaze danced high into the air and the embers at the bottom burned hot.

She approached quietly, not wanting to startle the dragon from his slumber.

She made her way around his body, his back rising and falling with each breath.

Without opening his eyes, he whispered, "What is it that you want from me, Princess?"

Shyeanna made her way closer to the red dragon, and put her hand on his huge scaled arm.

"I need your help," she said. "I need to know everything you know about my uncle."

Garille opened one eye and looked at her.

"He was jealous of your father and he was evil," he growled. "What else is there to know about him?"

"Why was he jealous?" Shyeanna asked. "I need to know the whole story."

Garille lifted his head and stared at the girl. She was a teenager now and she was even more beautiful than she had been as a child.

"Did your father not tell you?" Garille asked.

"My father never told me anything. He refused to talk about any of it," Shyeanna said. "No one else will talk about him either. No one will tell me anything. I need to know."

Garille groaned and sat up to his full twelve feet of height and stretched. His wings spread as far as they could in the cramped cave and he looked down at the girl again.

"If your father won't tell you anything," the dragon said. "Then it is not my place to say."

"My father is dead," Shyeanna said.

The expression on Garille's face changed from annoyance to surprise and then to sorrow.

"I hadn't heard," he said. "I'm so sorry."

"That's why I need your help," Shyeanna said. "I need you to tell me what happened."

"Because now," Garille said sadly. "Your uncle is trying to kill you."

"Yes," she answered. "So you know why?"

"He wants power," Garille said. "He thinks the throne is rightfully his. Which, technically, he has a claim to it. Especially with your father dead."

"Why?" she asked.

"I'm sure you are looking for more than the obvious answer of the fact that he was the eldest son," Garille said.

"I know that he was passed over by my grandfather," Shyeanna said. "But I don't know why."

"Wouldn't that be enough to make you angry?" Garrille asked.

"Well, yes," Shyeanna said. "But there is more to the story, and I need to know it. He seems to be very determined to kill me."

The dragon sighed.

"The truth will make things more complicated for you," Garille said. "Not easier."

"That's why I need to know it," she said.

"There is one fact that is being hidden, not just by your father," Garille said. "By others in the kingdom. It is a secret that no one wants to tell, because no one wants your uncle to be king."

"Please tell me," she begged. "I cannot fight him if I don't know the facts."

Garille growled low and slow.

"You may not fight him at all once you know the truth," Garille whispered. "You are too much like your father. Your integrity will win out."

"Tell me," she demanded.

"You are not of royal blood," Garille said in almost a whisper.

"What?" Shyeanna gasped.

"You were adopted," Garille said. "You have no legal claim to the throne."

"So I'm not really queen," Shyeanna said slowly.

She let the words sink in. The shock of her father's lie was almost too much to bear. Then, as she realized that the only blood heir was her uncle, the horror started. She felt the terror clench deep in her chest and she momentarily gasped for air.

"My uncle cannot be king," she whispered.

"Technically he doesn't have a legal claim either," Garille said. "Because he was disowned."

"So who is to be the ruler of Shal Tahl?" she asked.

"You have two choices," Garille said.

"Which are?"

"You can keep the secret," he said. "No other land knows of your blood line. They will all accept you as Queen."

"Who are my real parents?" she asked. "My family?"

"They were killed in the battle of the marshes," Garille said. "They were fleeing when they died. Your father, DaeMark, tried to defend them, but he was too late. Your mother asked him to care for you. So he did. He raised you as his own. He said he was your natural father and that your mother had died in childbirth.The kingdom fell in love with you. Those in the know kept your secret, since there was no other heir."

Shyeanna stood silently as she let it all wash over her. The fact that her entire life was a lie and that others knew.

"How did Zalta bond with me then?" Shyeanna asked. "Dragons can only bond with those of royal blood."

Garille stared at her for a long time, "That is a question that no one can answer. Zalta is rare, a combination of two breeds of dragon. She should not have been able to bond with anyone. She would be considered an outsider among the dragons, if it were not for you."

Shye considered Zalta. She had always been proud that her dragon was different. That she was odd among her peers. She had never considered the fact that otherwise, Zalta would be ostracized.

"What is my other choice?" she asked.

"It will be hard," Garille said. "And you will not like it."

"Tell me," she said.

"There is another line," Garille said. "A child was taken away when he was young. Everyone was told he died at birth."

"What?" Shyeanna said. "I have another uncle?"

"From generations back, yes," Garille nodded. "He was taken away. Somewhere safe. In case of this very scenario."

"They planned for this?" she asked.

"There were prophecies," the dragon said. "So yes, they planned for this. Generations ago."

"Where do I find him?" Shyeanna asked.

"Which dragons have never been bonded to the royal family?" Garille asked.

"The yellow dragons of the desert," she said.

"Why do you think that is?" Garille asked.

"They chose not to participate," she shrugged. "They don't like the woodland and wet terrain of Shal Tahl."

Garille shook his head. "They have been raising the hidden line of the royal family. If you choose to give up your throne, then you must find the hidden line. You must find the new heir."

Shyeanna stood quietly and considered her options.

"If the other kingdoms found out that I have no royal blood, what would they do?" Shyeanna asked.

Garille shrugged. "It depends. If they liked you, some might consider the adoption as making you the legal heir. Some would declare war to take over the kingdom. Some would demand someone with royal blood take over, thinking it could damage their claims on their own thrones if Shal Tahl allowed a tainted bloodline on the throne."

"I am not tainted," she said.

"Oh but you are," Garille said. "With no legal claim to the throne. So you must consider your options carefully. Threats of war could make your loyal subjects suddenly demand your head to save their sons."

"Come back with me," she said.

"What?" Garille raised his head. "No."

"You have to," she said. "I need you. I need your counsel."

Garille sighed. "I can't. My shame is too great."

"Yes, you can," a voice from behind Shyeanna said.

The silver dragon came from out of the shadows and stared at Garille.

"If I can face the shame of being a half-breed, you can face the shame of Talask's betrayal," Zalta said. "Come back with us."

"No," Garille snapped, smoke trailing from his nostrils.

Zalta straightened as much as she could in the cramped cave and drew her head and chest up.

"Garille, for now, Shyeanna is the Queen of Shal Tahl," Zalta said in her most authoritative voice. "That means, that I am the Queen's Bonded Dragon. You are under my authority and I command you to come back home to the castle to face your punishment. Have some dignity and comply."

Garille lowered his head to the younger dragon, "What will be my punishment, if I go?"

Zalta narrowed her eyes at the red dragon, "You will go, and when we return home with you, you are to serve your time as a Dragon Member of the Royal Council and advise the Queen on matters of State until she releases you or relinquishes her throne."

Shyeanna could feel her dragon shaking behind her.

Garille sighed. "Or until she is killed and her throne is taken forcefully by her uncle."

"So be it," Shyeanna said suddenly. "I will stay in control of Shal Tahl until death or a new heir is found. Either way, I will not abandon Shal Tahl and leave her to my uncle without a fight."

She reached behind her and rested her hand on Zalta's leg for encouragement. Her scales were cold and the young dragon was still shaking.

"Are you coming willingly?" Zalta asked. "Or will I have to take you by force?"

Garille chuckled. "You are half my size, child," he said to Zalta. "I admire your courage. You will serve the Queen well."

Garille stood in a crouch in the cave and faced them. "Very well, lead me home and to my punishment."

He bent his neck down and looked Shyeanna directly in the eyes. She could feel his hot breath on her face.

He stared into her eyes for a moment, as though he could see into her soul, and said, "Long live the Queen."

SHYEANNA TRUDGED THROUGH the forest. Zalta led the way in front of her, and Garille brought up the rear behind her. Shyeanna bore the terrain without complaint, her dress muddy and wet up to her knees as she made her way through under the canopy of wet and dripping trees. The rain had made for slick muddy ground as they walked.

The sun was getting low and Shyeanna knew that they would not make it back before dark. The darkness caused by the trees was already thickening and making it hard for her to see the rough terrain beneath her feet. She stumbled along, trying to push forward. The thoughts in her head led her to one conclusion.

That meant camping in the forest. Something she was not fond of in the best of circumstances. She was cold and tired and not looking forward to sleeping on the freezing cold ground.

In the clearing ahead, she could hear bickering voices. She smiled when she recognized them as her friends. She pushed her way through to the clearing, following the flickering fire light and the familiar voices. She breathed in the wonderful smell of fresh stew and basked in the warm glow of a roaring fire.

"How did you find us?" Shyeanna said as she approached a small dwarf who was stirring the stew over the edge of the fire.

"Shyeanna!" the dwarf exclaimed. "I mean, Your Majesty. I won't ever get used to that, you know."

"You won't have to," Garille said from behind her.

"Oh shut your mouth," Zalta snapped. "We don't need your pessimism."

The silver dragon walked over to a short tree with lavender colored leaves and ivy that wrapped its way up the trunk. She nuzzled her face into the velvety leaves.

The tree reached out two branches and hugged the dragon back.

"It's good to see you, Burble, Crawl," Zalta said.

"I see the Velvet Tree and its symbiote are still with you," Garille said.

"We would never leave the Princess," the ivy said. "I mean, the Queen."

Shyeanna smiled.

Burble, the Velvet Tree, and Crawl, the Crawling Ivy that lived on Burble, had been with her as long as she could remember. They babysat her when the King was busy, and played with her throughout her childhood.

She was probably the only child who grew up having a tree for a best friend. Burble was a magical Purple Velvet tree. He could walk, talk, and his leaves were of a magic velvet fiber that, with the right skills, could be sewn together to make a seamless fabric. The cloth was quite valuable.

That was where the dwarf came in. Rumtuskin had also been with Shye as long as she could remember. He had the magical skills necessary to make the seamless cloth. He was a master tailor and had, arguably, the best skills in the lands.

Usually, the Crawling Ivy symbiote would not let anyone near their velvet trees. The Crawling Ivy kept their Velvet Trees alive. They leeched the sap of the tree for sustenance. A sap, which if left untapped, would kill the tree. They were also fiercely loyal to their trees and would strangle anyone or anything that threatened their food source. The Ivy was very fast and could shoot out several yards to defend their tree from any attacker.

Normally, no one could get near enough to the trees to harvest the leaves for use, but Burble had allergies. To everything. So when he sneezed, he lost leaves. Rumtuskin would gather the leaves and use them to make his magical cloth. In exchange, he was also a guardian of Burble, in tandem with Crawl.

The three were inseparable.

Five, including Shyeanna and Zalta. They were closer than family. They would all defend one another with their lives.

Shyeanna felt confident that her friends would serve as great council to her as Queen, for however long she may reign.

"So I see you agreed to come," Rumtuskin said to Garille. "I didn't think you would."

"You owe me some spring water," Burble said to the dwarf. "I knew he'd come."

"I wasn't going to," Garille said. "But the dragon pup was quite convincing."

"Don't call me a pup," Zalta snapped. "I am your superior, in every way."

Garille sucked in his breath and let it come out his nose in smoke. He bit his tongue before he said something he would regret.

Zalta waited for the verbal attack to come from the pure bred dragon, but it didn't come.She looked at Garille with a new respect. Most dragons would have responded. She was still new to her post as a bonded dragon, as well as the first and only half-breed.

It was an extremely controversial bonding. There had been whispers among the dragons as well as among the humans. Could a half-breed dragon even bond? And for those in the know, would it work at all with an adopted child of the king, half-breed or not?

The fact that the bonding worked settled some of the whispers. Some thought that meant that Shyeanna had some royal blood in her after all. Others thought that just meant that the Crystal Tower had accepted her as the heir to the throne.

The fact that it was with a half-breed dragon. That set off even more whispers. Was Zalta special? Could any half-breed bond? What was it about Zalta that made the bonding successful?

Shyeanna chose Zalta herself. There was normally a ritual that happened where the parents have a large say in the choice of the bonding dragon. That ritual did not happen. Shyeanna's real parents were dead. There was no queen, and DaeMark, the King, the only father she knew, had left the choice of dragon in Shyeanna's hands. He felt that her relationship with her bonded dragon was more important than any ritual.

Zalta had been an assistant at the white dragons' training school. She had not been allowed to train herself, but she knew everything that was being taught. Better than most of the white dragon students.

She had been expelled from being an assistant in the training camp. She knew too much and had become a distraction to some of the students. They resented the fact that she was present at all and there was bullying among them. Zalta was the victim, but since she wasn't eligible, according to dragon standards, she was the one expelled.

Zalta had come to the castle after seeking permission to attend a dragon camp from her father's tribe. The black dragons had flat refused to accept her. Her father had never even come to see her.

So her only option was to go to the castle and seek permission from the crown. She knew it was a long shot, but it was her last resort.

That was where she met Burble and Crawl. They were out in front of the castle, sunning themselves. When they saw the silver dragon approach, they greeted her kindly.

When she told them of her plight, they introduced her directly to Shyeanna.

From the moment Zalta and Shyeanna met, they both knew. Between the immediate chemistry and the friendship that developed between the two, Shyeanna refused to consider any of the other dragon candidates.

The choice had already been made.

When the day of the bonding came, people from all over ShalTahl came to watch. It was usual for many of the kingdom to come to see a bonding, they happened so rarely.

This one was different. For those who knew, the fact that the princess was not of true royal blood was a draw. For everyone else, since the dragon was a half-breed, some came just to see if it would work. If the Crystal Tower would truly accept the bonding, or if they would be rejected.

It had happened once before. An adopted prince, long ago, had tried to bond with a dragon. The tower didn't accept them. Everyone expected some sort of big reaction, but the rejection was silent. A quiet refusal by the tower that shattered the hopes of the young prince. Of one day becoming king. The dragon was shamed and set into hiding. He never wanted to be seen or heard from again.

So when the day came for Shyeanna and Zalta, some people came to see them be bonded. Some came to see if it would work. A failed bonding meant more than shame for just the dragon. No heir to the throne wanted a failed bonding, especially not when Shyeanna had chosen the dragon herself.

Thousands of people came to the ceremony.

No one was disappointed.

Shyeanna and Zalta had no doubts about the bonding working. They knew in their hearts that they were meant to bond together and were to take the place of the king and his loyal dragon.

One unknowingly adopted, and one a half-breed.

The moment of a successful bonding, the Crystal Tower grows. Mild earthquakes shake the earth, thunder and lightning are common. The Tower shakes and rattles and the Crystal grows and adds on an addition to the castle that becomes the new living quarters for the bonded and their dragon.

When the day came for Shyeanna and Zalta's bonding, the earthquakes were severe. The castle grew massively. The Tower not only accepted them, but did so with open arms. An additional room was added, beyond what was normal. It was specially made for Zalta. As a silver dragon, she had special needs. A closeness to nature was more necessary for her survival. The new room was a massive greenhouse, complete with a waterfall and natural gardens. It was the first time in centuries that a ground floor addition was made in the Tower. So that the plants in the greenhouse could grow from the ground itself.

The nation celebrated that day. The Crystal Tower's acceptance of Shyeanna bonding to Zalta assuaged many fears. No one in the land wanted the king's brother to take the throne. The Tower agreed.

Shyeanna's secret was still safe.

As for the other lands, as far as they were concerned, the new heir of Shal Tahl had been officially chosen.

Garille had secretly come to see the bonding. He was one that thought it would fail. He hoped in his heart that it would work, but he was privy to the secret that had been kept. He was waiting to see if the half-breed would need sanctuary. He had been willing to take her in if necessary.

He hadn't needed to.

Watching the Tower grow that day had hardened his heart slightly. It had made his failure as a bonded dragon more acute. More rare. More real.

He left when the celebrating began. He had vowed to himself to never return.

Garille was breaking that vow, but only to stop Talask from whatever he had planned.

He watched the small group as they sat around the warmth of the fire. The dwarf serving soup to the new Queen as she sat in the mud next to her half-breed dragon.

The Velvet tree sat beside the dragon, with his leaves and branches draped over her. The equivalent to having an arm around a friend. At the same time, giving much needed energy from nature to the silver dragon.

Crawl, wrapped tightly around Burble's trunk, snored quietly as he slept soundly. The darkness that surrounded them his cue for slumber.

Garille smiled slightly at the closeness of the small family. He watched as the Queen would occasionally touch Zalta's arm or snuggle in closer to her dragon. Zalta's eyelids started to droop and she turned her face towards the Queen as she curled up for sleep. The bonding between them was much more than magical. It was unconditional love and trust.

Garille had never had that kind of closeness with Talask.

Never in recorded history had one of the Royal Family gone so bad. The evil that grew in Talask's heart had even started to corrupt the Crystal Tower. Their section of the Tower had started to turn black, making their portion looked charred, burnt. Leaving a permanent scar on the Tower itself.

When Garille left in his shame, he couldn't look back. He couldn't bear to see the damage that he had done to the Tower. It could be seen for miles. His failure marked on the Royal Domicile for everyone to see. Forever.

Garille winced at the thought of parents explaining his failure to their children when they came to see the once beautiful Crystal Tower, only to see the charred scar of a failed dragon. The parents would tell them of how Talask had gone bad. How Garille was shamed. How his name would only be remembered in the wake of the lessons of failure.

Garille rested his head on the ground. He longed to come over to the circle of light around the fire and share in the feeling of family that the others shared so easily.

Once again, he reminded himself that he was an outsider. He didn't belong. He never did. The rejection of the Tower proving his banishment.

Shyeanna listened to the slight snoring that whistled softly from Zalta and chuckled to herself. She handed her empty bowl to Rumtuskin, who took it happily and refilled it for himself.

The Queen looked around and saw that Garille had once again separated himself out and was laying in the shadows of the edge of the woods.

She stood up and walked towards the red dragon.

"I'm sure you would be much happier to be over by the bonfire," she said to him.

"I don't belong," Garille said softly.

"That's not true," Shyeanna said. "As far as I'm concerned, you are still part of the Royal Family. Please come to the warmth of the fire. A red dragon is much more subject to hypothermia this time of year."

Garille looked longingly at the circle of warm light that surrounded the fire.

"If it helps," she said. "As your Queen, I command you to come into the light of the fire."

He looked at her. Her command was one of compassion, not anger.

He slowly got to his feet and followed the young Queen closer to the flames.

Garille set himself down on the opposite side of the group. In the light and warmth of the fire, he followed the Queen's command to the word, if not the intention.

Shyeanna let him get comfortable before she went over and sat down next to him.

She faced the red dragon, one side of her face lit brightly by the fire, one side hidden in the shadows of the darkness. Garille thought she looked beautiful by the firelight, and regal befitting her station.

She reached out and set a hand on his front claw. He resisted the urge to pull away. It had been what seemed like forever since he had last had human contact. As a bonded dragon, failed or not, he longed for it. But he still didn't feel worthy.

"You are part of this family," she said to him softly. "We will fix things. You do not have to be remembered as a failure. You can be remembered as a hero. As the one who helped bring Talask to justice. The Tower can be repaired."

"The scar will always be there," Garille said. "It will always be a reminder of my shame."

Shyeanna shook her head, "I don't believe that. It can become so much more. Just like you can. You just can't give up. You can't hide anymore. You must come home and repair the damage. Only you can do that."

Garille stared at her tiny hand, still resting on his claw. She seemed so small and fragile, yet she was much stronger than he felt.

"You don't know the evil that Talask possesses," Garille whispered. "I've seen it. I've felt it. His evil crawls inside my brain like frost taking over a field."

"With family, you have the sun that will melt that frost," she said. "Together we are stronger than he is. You are stronger than he is. We can do this together."

Garille stared into the Queen's eyes. He remembered when she was a baby, she looked at him with the same love and amazement. As a child, those blue eyes were filled with tears and pain when he chose to leave. She had always touched his heart with those eyes. Like the clear blue of a bright sunny day. He had a softness for her that he had for no one else, and it came from those eyes.

Now, as almost an adult, she had the same power over him. He glanced at Zalta, pushing back the wave of jealousy that he could feel rising in his chest.

He had trained for so long to become a bonded dragon. He wondered if it was bad luck or fate that had determined that he be matched with Talask. The good fortune that Zalta had with being bonded with Shyeanna. They should have failed the bonding process, but by fate or good fortune, or whatever forces were at work, they were successful. Garille could tell by watching them that the two would rule well together, and he hoped they kept the crown.

Garille looked into her eyes.

"What happens to me if we defeat him?" Garille asked.

"It depends on what you mean by defeat," Shyeanna said.

They both knew what he meant.

Dragons had a much longer lifespan than humans, but bonded dragons were tied to their human's life. If the human died an unnatural death, the dragon died too. Only a natural death releases the dragon from the bond.

A great number of dragons were so distraught by their bonded human's death, that they died shortly after anyway. Most say of a broken heart.

It is the price they pay to have the honor of serving the Crystal Tower.

It was a price paid willingly by the dragons for centuries. It was the bonding that brought peace between humans and dragons. It was the creation of the Crystal Tower that holds the bonds. It is the only land that has a tower.

Shal Tahl is the land that holds the magic. It is the land where people come for peace. It is the place that Talask wants to destroy.

Garille knew that all that stood between Talask and him destroying the Tower, was himself and the young woman in front of him. They were the only ones who could save the Tower. It could mean his death.

No dragon had ever had to fight their bonded human before. As he watched Shyeanna and Zalta interact over the evening, he hoped it would never have to happen again.

"Thank you for coming with us," she said. "I know this is difficult for you."

"You have no idea," Garille said.

Shyeanna kissed the red dragon on the nose and placed her hand lovingly on his snout.

She then went and laid down on the small bed that Rumtuskin had made for her near the fire.

After Shyeanna fell asleep, Zalta made her way over to Garille's side and quietly laid down next to him.

"I've always been jealous of you," Zalta whispered as she gazed at Shyeanna.

"You have been jealous of me?" Garille said in amazement.

"You were there for her as a child," Zalta said. "You got to see her grow up. I didn't get to see that."

"Only because Talask shunned me," Garille said softly. "She took pity on me and spent time with me."

"It wasn't pity," Zalta said. "It was love. It is love. You and she have a relationship that I will never know. You helped raise her. You should be proud of that."

Garille looked over at the young Queen who was now sound asleep. Rumtuskin was sitting near her, working his magic on some of the leaves that Burble had sneezed off of himself. The dwarf was deep in the process of making a warmer blanket to cover the Queen for the cold night that was coming.

"I had never thought about it that way," Garille said.

"Maybe you should," Zalta said. "Maybe instead of feeling sorry for yourself because Talask was a failure that was out of your control. You should look at the success you had with the upbringing of the new Queen and the hand you did have in that."

Garille looked back at Zalta. She had tears forming in the corners of her eyes and her voice quivered as she spoke.

"Maybe your only real failure was that you quit and hid yourself away when the Crystal Tower needed you most," she said. "At least that is a failure that can be fixed."

Garille stared into the eyes of the silver dragon who was fighting to hold his gaze. She wasn't used to telling off a dragon that, under normal circumstances, would be her mentor and superior.

He wasn't qualified at this moment, and she was right.

"You are wise beyond your years, little one," he said to her.

"And you are wise with experience," she said. "We need that right now."

"Am I correct to assume that Dargon-" Garille choked on the words.

Zalta nodded. "The day after the King."

The majestic black dragon had been his best friend. Dargon and Garille had been bonded to the two royal brothers on the same day. The human brothers were twins, and the red and the black dragon had become closer than brothers. They came up together in their training and they grew up together in the Tower.

The only thing harder than leaving the young princess behind had been leaving Dargon. He never had the chance to even say goodbye. Now he would never have the chance to apologize.

Garille hung his head. He didn't want Zalta to see him cry.

"There's no shame in crying," Zalta whispered. "I loved him to. He was like a father to me during the time I knew him. He didn't hesitate for a moment to take me on as a pupil."

Dargon was the one thing that had made Garille think that he could handle going back to the Tower. Now he was gone, and Garille would have to face things alone.

"Marsa is still there," Zalta said. "If that helps."

Garille lifted his head and stared at the silver dragon.

"Marsa still lives?"

"She does," Zalta nodded.

Marsa was a rarity. Not just because she was a green dragon bonded to a Queen, but because she had outlived her Queen.

Mattaea had died years before, but Marsa lived on. She had been like a mother to both Dargon and himself.

He had been close with her too. Which was also a rarity. Red and green dragons had an uneasy peace at best, but the fire dragon and the forest dragon had been able to put their clans' animosity aside to be able to work together for the sake of the Crystal Tower.

THE UNEVENTFUL NIGHT led all of them to sleep peacefully except for Garille.

The red dragon had used his sleeplessness as an excuse to keep watch, but there was nothing in the darkness of the forest that was a danger. Two dragons near a large fire seemed to be a deterrent for most large beasts that may have wandered close by. None decided to take on the dragon who had forgone sleep.

Garille kept the fire going and watched the smoke rise into the darkness while the others slept. The Queen slept peacefully, even through the dwarf's snoring and the velvet tree's occasional sneezing and sniffling. The ivy was silent, but was vigilant through the night also.

Garille had been uneasy all night long. He was nervous about going back to the Crystal Tower. He had not seen the Tower nor the land of Shal Tahl for years. He wasn't looking forward to seeing his scar on the otherwise beautiful Tower.

When morning came, Zalta awoke early and wandered into the forest. She returned with some fish and several rabbits and set a few of them before the dwarf.

Rumtuskin eagerly set about making some breakfast out of the fresh meat.

Zalta then headed over to Garille and gave the red dragon a few critters of his own.

"If you want more, we can hunt together," Zalta said. "For something bigger."

"This is fine, thank you," Garille said, ignoring the grumbling in his stomach. "I can wait until we are back in Shal Tahl for more."

Zalta nodded. Dragons could go longer than humans and dwarves without food. The snacks supplied by Zalta would be more than enough to hold them over.

The group ate breakfast without much talking, with only Burble's sneezes breaking the silence between them.

The birds of the forest were waking up and filling the air with the sounds of chirping and fluttering wings.

They put out the fire and cleaned up their campsite. Shyeanna wrapped herself in the new blanket that Rumtuskin had worked on the night before. The morning air was still crisp and chilly, and without the fire, she found herself getting cold.

After Rumtuskin was sure that he had cleaned up the cooking supplies and had picked up every last stray leaf from Burble, they were ready to set out for home.

GARILLE GREW MORE NERVOUS as they approached the Tower. With every step, his anxiety at facing his past grew heavier.

As they came near the end of the forest, he could see the glint of the sun on the Crystal occasionally through the trees. Blinding glints that penetrated the shadows in great flashes of light.

As they reached the end of the tree line, they could see over the town that surrounded the Tower. It was the land of Shal Tahl. The townspeople rushed up to greet their Queen and her search party. Garille was touched and greeted on all sides as he walked behind Zalta along the wide dirt road that led towards the Crystal Tower.

Garille tried to be polite and greet the townspeople. They ran over to the road on either side of him to cheer him on and to see him up close. Children ran alongside him as he walked because they wanted to touch his scales, but his attention kept being drawn away by the sight of the Tower.

It had been years since he had laid eyes on it and it was even more glorious than he remembered. The sun glinted off of the crystal and made rainbows within the crystal and shot small rainbows off of it in all directions. The clear, unflawed crystal was beautiful to behold. It was an amazing sight. With the exception of one single tower. It was marred black and looked like it had been burned out. A single black scar on what was otherwise the most beautiful building ever beheld.

The land of Shal Tahl was proud of their Tower. It was not man-made, but formed by magic. So no other land could begin to compete with their beautiful Tower. As they drew closer, Garille had a difficult time meeting the eyes of the loyal townspeople. He could not tear his eyes away from the single darkened tower that grew closer with each step.

In front of the main Tower was the large circle surrounded by gardens where all of the bondings took place. Garille wanted to side-step around it rather than walk through it, but Shyeanna walked straight through the path that led down the center of the circle and he didn't dare break stride with her.

When the party reached the center of the large bricked in circle, Shyeanna turned to address the crowd that had gathered to watch them return home with the long secluded dragon.

"Thank you all for coming," she said.

The crowd immediately silenced so they could hear the Queen's words.

"As you can see, we have found Garille," she was interrupted by cheers.

Zalta and Garille had moved quietly around so they were behind Shyeanna, with their backs to the Tower, facing the crowd with the Queen. Garille kept his head lowered, still reeling with the shame of his past, and now being forced to face a crowd that he suddenly felt that he was not ready to face.

Rumtuskin and Burble had moved to the edge of the circle, and left the royalty center stage.

"Garille has agreed to become an advisor to my council, to help us to maintain order, and, if necessary, to do battle with anyone who would try to usurp the crown."

The crowd cheered again.

"We now have our red dragon back at home where he belongs," Shyeanna continued. "I hope we can all welcome him warmly back into the family."

The crowd cheered louder and some people were throwing their hats into the air.

Garille felt it first. The ground began shaking under his feet.

Shyeanna and Zalta looked at one another and then over at Garille.

The people that had started encroaching into the circle immediately fell back into the crowd outside of the bonding circle.

The ground shook so hard that it knocked people at the edge of the circle off of their feet. Women grabbed their small children to keep them safe from falling to the brick walkways.

Shyeanna turned and looked up at the Tower.

The blackened tower was shaking violently. People near that end of the Crystal Tower ran from the fear of getting hit by falling crystal.

The black tower shattered and shot pieces of crystal in all directions. The crowd ducked to avoid getting hit, but the shards evaporated and disintegrated into the air before any of the pieces hit the crowd.

Down on the first floor, where Shyeanna and Zalta's addition had been made, a new tower was sprouting. A new addition for Garille.

As the ground stopped shaking, Garille looked at the tower in amazement. The blackened tower was no more. Completely obliterated from the Crystal Tower. Gone forever.

A new bond had been made. The Crystal Tower had done something it had never done before. It broke a bond.

Garille could feel the freedom. He was released from the evil of Talask. No longer did he feel tied to the man that he had spent so much time trying to break away from.

He was now tied to the Queen.

The Tower had bonded him to her.

Shyeanna, the first Queen without a blood-line tie to the Tower, was now bonded to two dragons. Something that had never even been thought of, much less done.

The crowd went wild, the cheering was louder than before and people were embracing and dancing through the bonding circle to celebrate the new spontaneous bonding.

They had just witnessed history being made. There was a new confidence that their adversary could now be overcome.

Zalta approached Garille and looked him in the eyes.

Garille immediately lowered his head, in a bow to his superior.

Zalta reached out with a front claw and lifted his face so that he was staring into her eyes.

"Can you feel it?" Zalta asked.

"What?" Garille asked. He was so overwhelmed that he didn't know what he was feeling anymore.

"We're bonded also," Zalta said.

THE INDIGO-EYED PUP

Nicolas woke to the sound of hunters calling out to one another in the darkness. At first, he tried to sleep through it, rolling over and trying to kick the too short blanket over his feet. But it was no use, if he pulled the blanket up high, it left his feet uncovered. If he pulled it lower on the bed with his toes, to cover his feet, his shoulders lay exposed to the cold.

It wasn't the first time the hunters had been on his land, and he usually didn't mind. They kept the predators' numbers down and kept the deer from eating all of his herb garden.

He tried to go back to sleep, but the yelping of the great wolves roused him from the semi-warmth of his bed.

This would not do.

Nicolas swung his feet over the side of the bed and waved his hand in the pitch black that filled his hut.

Several candles lit around the room, giving him enough light to see by.

He slid his feet into his slippers and felt his joints ache in the cold biting air. He reached to the end of his bed and pulled on his fur-lined robe. It didn't make his old aching joints feel any better, but it kept the bite of the night air off of his skin.

He stood up and shuffled across the room, letting the wooden floorboards help him get his slippers all the way settled on his feet.

He picked up a lantern and it lit as he touched it.

The papers from his latest project lay strewn all over the table. As he picked up the lantern, a few pages fluttered to the floor. He made a mental note to organize his table so he could find the things he needed when the time came to conduct his experiments.

But there was a more pressing need at the moment. The need for the final piece to his upcoming work. The final piece that would lead to his own end, and a new beginning.

He went to the door and opened it.

A rush of cold air hit him as the outside air tried to make its way inside the hut. The smell of the conifer trees helped to wake him up, as the fresh smell of trees always did. He found forest living to be quite invigorating.

He pulled his robe tighter around himself and waved his hand at the fireplace from the doorway.

He must have been asleep for a long while to let the fire go down. But that was usually the result of one of his visions. He could have been asleep for days at this point. He was just happy he hadn't frozen to death in the meantime.

But he knew that no matter how long he slept, he wouldn't have died. Because this was the night the visions spoke of, he was sure of it. The visions were never wrong.

He stepped out into the darkness and listened carefully.

The hunters were not too far to the west of him, and they were in pursuit.

The yelps and growls of the wolves told him that the hunters had gotten one. Most likely the mother. She was the first to die in his visions.

He could hear the pups as the hunters got them as well.

Nicolas knew he had to move quickly.

He ran off his tiny porch in front of his little hut and out into the darkness. Towards the sounds of the hunters.

The ground was hard and cold beneath his slippers and he lost his footing more times than he would have liked.

He grumbled to himself, wishing he had taken the time to put on his boots. But in his sleep-filled hurry, he hadn't thought about it until it was now too late to go back for them.

Nicolas could hear the pup already. He had to find him.

This pup would be the last of his kind, and the gods had great things in store for him.

He made his way to the edge of the woods that surrounded his tiny wooden hut.

The coniferous trees were calling to him. Instructing him where to go to find the pup. They led him further into the darkness and closer to the hunters.

He could hear the hunters battling the adult wolves of the pack.

And he knew that the wolves would lose.

The humans had been at odds with the wrong wolves.

The gray wolves were the ones sneaking into the villages at night, stealing small children from their beds. But the humans had no cares about whether or not they were hunting down the wrong wolves. They wanted to hunt them all, the great black wolves included.

Nicolas held up his lantern. He could hear two pups coming his way.

The small black creatures ran straight towards him and his lantern light.

Nicolas held the lantern high and looked for the sign that his vision had shown him.

The first pup came towards him and looked up at him with dark brown frightened eyes.

A smaller pup came up behind him.

He held the lantern down towards them both.

The smaller one looked up at him as if he had known Nicolas for ages. The iridescent indigo eyes stared up at him and he nearly jumped into the old man's arms.

Nicolas picked up the indigo eyed pup.

He could hear the hunters coming their way.

"Another one went this way," he could hear them calling to one another.

He looked at the brown eyed pup.

"May your sacrifice someday be worth it," Nicolas said to the pup on the ground. "I'm so sorry."

He turned and headed back to his hut with the indigo-eyed pup.

The other pup tried to follow, but he was too tired and couldn't keep up with the wizard's long strides.

He left the pup behind, without looking back, and extinguishing his lantern, he disappeared into the darkness.

The hunters found the pup moments later and the pack was brought to an end. Or so the hunters thought.

Nicolas went into his hut with tears in his eyes and looked down at the indigo-eyed pup that he held in his arms. He listened to the hunters congratulating themselves on ending the threat of the wolves. As they headed back towards the town, they began to sing a victory cheer, not knowing that one single pup had managed to escape.

"You are now the last of your kind," Nicolas said.

The pup wiggled closer to Nicolas's chest for warmth.

"Your destiny is now set in motion."

IT HAD BEEN SEVERAL months since the hunters had ended the great black wolves and hunted them to extinction.

With the exception of the indigo-eyed pup that Nicolas had been secretly raising.

The gray wolves had moved on, as they always did, and the humans foolishly congratulated themselves on ending the wolf threat on their village.

But Nicolas knew better.

He knew the gray wolves would someday return.

But that wasn't his concern.

His concern was that now, the destiny of many relied on the survival of the indigo-eyed pup.

Nicolas had been leaving the pup alone in his hut for a short time now and then. Gradually lengthening his departures for longer and longer periods of time. When he was sure the pup could be left alone without howling for a matter of hours, Nicolas made his first venture into town in months. Or possibly years.

There were supplies he needed.

He entered the small town and was alarmed at how crowded it was growing.

The edges of the town reached further into the forest than he remembered and as he made his way through the hustle and bustle of the busy streets, it was a while before he saw anything familiar. It wasn't until he reached the merchant streets that things started looking the way he recognized what was once a very small town.

He entered the herbalist's shop and a small bell filled the air with a metallic jingle and announced his presence. His nose was greeted by the familiar scents of many herbs and spices, most of which he was very familiar with. It smelled like the comfort of home to him.

The shopkeeper, MacMillian, came out from the back and smiled when he saw Nicolas.

"Long time no see, old man," MacMillian said cheerfully.

"You're one to talk," Nicolas said.

MacMillian was starting to show his age. His hair was longer and grayer than the last time Nicolas had been here. And the wrinkles on his face were deeper and more pronounced than Nicolas remembered them being.

"How long has it been?" Nicolas asked.

He no longer trusted his own sense of time. He had been alone in the forest for too long.

"I haven't seen you in at least two years," MacMillian said. "Maybe even three now."

"Has it been that long?" Nicolas muttered. "Seems like it's only been as many months."

"Time blends together when you live out in the wilds," MacMillian said.

"So, it does," Nicolas said.

He walked up to the counter and placed a neatly written list before MacMillian.

"This is what I need," Nicolas said.

"That's quite a list," MacMillian said as he read down through the items.

"Like you said," Nicolas said. "It's been almost three years."

"I can get you all of these," MacMillian said. "But it will take me some time."

"I will stop in at the grocer's and come back then," Nicolas said.

"I'll have it ready by the time you return," MacMillian said as he started scurrying around to gather the items.

Nicolas waved and headed out the door. The jingle of the bell filled the air once again and Nicolas made his way out onto the busy street.

The smell of mud and horses assailed his nose.

He made his way down the bustling street and went into the grocer's market. He didn't recognize anyone who worked there, so he busied himself gathering his own items.

Flour, sugar, and other things he needed piled into his basket. He took it all up to the counter and the merchant added up his purchases.

Nicolas quietly paid and left quickly.

No one but the merchant seemed aware of his presence. And Nicolas had intended it to be that way.

Within minutes, the only record or memory the merchant would have of Nicolas' visit would be the receipt for the purchases that lay in the stack on the counter.

Nicolas went back to the herbalist's shop and MacMillian was just finishing up his order when he came through the jingling door.

"I'm just finishing up the last of it," MacMillian said.

He tucked a few brown paper wrapped items on top of the pile.

Nicolas looked at his groceries and the wrapped packages on the counter and wondered how he would manage to carry all of it home.

"I'll get you another basket," MacMillian said.

The gray headed man slipped into the back and reemerged with a basket that he started filling with all of Nicolas's order.

"Thank you kindly," Nicolas said. "I didn't realize how much I would be buying today."

Nicolas opened the bag on his hip and looked at the remaining coins inside.

"How much do I owe you?" Nicolas asked.

"Your money's no good here, old man," MacMillian said.

Nicolas looked up at the man and blinked blankly. "What do you mean?"

MacMillian leaned over the counter and gestured for Nicolas to come closer.

Nicolas stepped up to the counter and leaned his ear towards the shopkeeper.

"You're not the only one with visions," MacMillian said.

Nicolas stepped back and looked at MacMillian. He could feel a cold shiver run through his body.

"What do you know?" Nicolas asked.

"I know nothing," MacMillian smiled at Nicolas and shrugged. "I did, however, add a large bone with lots of marrow to your order. Just in case the need for its use arises."

Nicolas stared at MacMillian, still not knowing what to make of the situation. The possession of a black wolf could mean imprisonment or death. He did not like the fact that someone else might know of the indigo-eyed pup's existence.

"Don't worry, your secret is safe with me," MacMillian said. "Don't think that you are alone in this. I have my part to play as well. Just know that if danger comes, you have a friend."

"Thank you," Nicolas said. He stared at MacMillian for a moment longer before nodding and saying again, "Thank you."

Nicolas took the basket off the counter and headed out of the shop, one basket over the crook of each arm.

He set out onto the bustling street once again, wishing that the town hadn't grown so much since his last visit.

He made his way to the edge of town and sat to rest for a moment before heading back to his hut in the center of the forest.

He thought about the words of his friend, McMillian.

Nicolas wondered who else might have visions beside him. And if they would all be allies, or if some would some be a threat to him and the pup.

He gathered his belongings and headed back on his way into the forest.

Nicolas was so lost in thought, he didn't realize that there was a flock of silent crows following him home.

WHEN NICOLAS ARRIVED back at his hut, the pup leapt to his feet when the old man came in through the door.

The puppy was getting rather large and was wagging his long black tail with happiness that the man was home. Nicolas was thrilled to see that everything in his hut was intact, and that the wolf had been well behaved while he was out.

Nicolas set his baskets on the table and then pet the wolf happily. He gave the wolf a solid pat on the back and then turned to the herbalist's basket.

"I think there might be a present here for you, Indigo," Nicolas said.

He rummaged around until he found the bone shaped package.

Indigo's eyes widened when he smelled the package and snatched the brown paper wrapped parcel out of Nicolas's hands before he could get the paper off.

Nicolas watched with amusement as Indigo took it to his favorite spot in front of the fireplace and tore the paper off with glee.

Nicolas laughed as the dog made a mess of the paper and then laid down on it as if it didn't exist to start in on his bone.

"Why don't you take that outside?" Nicolas suggested, opening the door for the wolf.

Indigo picked up the bone and ran through the door and, after doing a short amount of business, laid down on the porch happily, gnawing away at the bone.

Nicolas propped the door open so he could keep an eye on the pup and started to pick up the pieces of brown paper that the dog had strewn around on the floor. He was about to throw the paper into the fire when he noticed that there was writing on some of it.

He hadn't noticed the writing before, because the writing had been on the inside of the wrapping paper.

Nicolas found all of the pieces with writing and sat down at the table to piece the message together.

The message was short, but direct. And Nicolas was certain that it came from MacMillian, the herbalist, to him.

It said:

Beware the crows. They report back to one who should not know.

Nicolas got up quickly and went outside.

He stood next to the pup while he happily gnawed on the bone, holding it steady with his front paws as if they were hands.

Nicolas looked around and saw several crows sitting on his fence that he had built to protect his herb garden. A few more sat in the conifer trees in the distance.

Nicolas raised his hands and chanted a few words in the old dialect.

The crows burst into flames and fizzled to the ground in a mist of black ash.

"Inside," he commanded the wolf. "Let's take that inside by the fire."

The pup obediently took the bone into the hut and laid down happily by the fire and continued gnawing on the bone.

The wizard glanced at the pieces of the note again and shook his head.

He gathered up the pieces of paper with the message on it and tossed them into the fire. His friend went to lengths to hide the message, so he wasn't about to leave evidence of it laying around.

Nicolas watched the pup as he continued gnawing on the bone, completely oblivious to everything else around him.

Nicolas went over to the table and started unloading his purchases. He lovingly took each item out of the baskets and laid them on the table.

He started to unwrap each item and took care as he put away the items that needed no preparation for storage. Once the flour, sugar, and other items were neatly in their places, he looked at the array of items that needed to be stored in a more magical manner.

He spent the afternoon preparing tinctures and storing the magical items in a proper manner for each one.

When he was done with that, there remained only a few items left on the table. He glanced up at the pup, who was now laying belly up by his bone, sound asleep and panting happily.

Nicolas started preparing the remaining ingredients for making tea.

This wasn't any ordinary tea, and Nicolas treated it as such. He carefully measured out the exact amounts of the different herbs and spices for the tea. He meticulously wrapped them in a cloth bundle and then took the kettle off the fire.

He poured the hot water into a clean bowl and then set the kettle aside. He put the little bundle of herbs into the tea and as it steeped, he chanted the words of a spell that he had been spending the last few months putting together and memorizing.

The smell of the tea was worse than he thought it would be. He hoped that wouldn't be a problem. He swirled the bag of herbs around clockwise before taking it out of the tea, wringing out as much water as he could, and then tossing the drained bag into the fire.

The bag went up into a puff of indigo smoke and the smoke drifted out of the fire and slowly wafted over to the wolf who was still asleep on the floor.

The smoke encircled the wolf and as it came up to the wolf's nose, the smoke slowly drifted up into the animal's nostrils as he breathed in the indigo smoke.

The wolf woke up and looked over at Nicolas with his indigo eyes.

"You need to drink this as well," Nicolas said to the wolf.

He picked up the bowl of tea and brought it over to the wolf and set it on the floor in front of him.

Indigo sat up and sniffed the bowl. He made a face, licking his nose and looking at Nicolas.

"I know it smells bad," Nicolas said. "But you need to drink it down. "

The wolf sniffed it again and looked at Nicolas.

"Go on," Nicolas said. "Drink up."

The wolf sighed and then set to lapping up the tea from the bowl.

He stopped several times to gag and lick his mouth distastefully. But after a few minutes, the wolf had emptied the bowl of the tea.

Nicolas picked up the bowl and set it on the table and then went back over to sit with the wolf in front of the fire.

The wolf gagged a few more times. Nicolas was afraid the wolf would throw up the tea, thus nullifying its effects, but the wolf managed to keep the tea down.

"It's all right," Nicolas stroked the wolf down the length of his long silky back. "The taste will go away soon, but the effects should be permanent."

The wolf gagged again and then looked up at Nicolas.

"That tasted terrible," the wolf said.

Nicolas stared at the wolf for a moment, in shock, and then began to laugh.

"It worked," he said gleefully.

"Of course it worked," Indigo said. "You've been laboring over that spell forever."

"You can talk," he grabbed Indigo by the head and scratched him behind the ears.

"I can talk?" Indigo repeated. He pulled his head away from Nicolas. "You can understand me?"

"Yes," Nicolas laughed and clapped his hands together. "Yes, I can understand you."

"Well, this just made things a lot easier," Indigo said.

"That, my dear pup," Nicolas smiled. "Was the point."

TIME PASSED AND NICOLAS spent his days teaching Indigo everything that the pup would need to know.

When he felt the pup was ready, he told him what really happened the night that Nicolas found Indigo and rescued him from the hunters.

It took Indigo some adjustment when he learned that he was the last of his kind, but Nicolas gave him the space he needed and time to grieve.

One evening, by the fire, as they shared a meal, Nicolas felt it was time to tell Indigo of his visions.

"There will come a time, in the near future, where you will be on your own," Nicolas said. "You will need to take what you have learned from me and seek out your own visions and follow them."

"I don't want to go without you," Indigo said. "Why can't you come with me/"

"I would if I could," Nicolas said. "But the visions have told me that you will be on your own. I must sacrifice myself to save you."

"No," Indigo shook his head. "I don't like this vision. I don't want any if that's what they say."

"You have no voice in the matter," Nicolas said. "The visions will always come true."

"Then I refuse to have any," Indigo said.

Nicolas laughed softly to himself, "If only it were that easy."

Indigo pricked up his ears and listened to the sounds of the forest outside.

"I hear more crows," he said.

"Beware the crows," Nicolas said. "They will betray you to those who wish you dead."

Indigo sighed. "There are so many of them."

"I know," Nicolas said. "Remember the chant I taught you. It will burn the ones who have been sent to harm you. The rest are just simple birds."

"I'll remember," Indigo said.

Nicolas reached down and scratched Indigo under the chin. The wolf lifted his nose high into the air and let the old man scratch him for as long as he would.

Nicolas stopped and pat Indigo on the head and looked down at the dog.

"I think it's time we got some sleep," he said.

He and the dog climbed onto the bed. Nicolas pulled the blanket close up around his shoulders and Indigo laid down on Nicolas's cold feet.

Nicolas sighed with happiness, even though he knew that tonight was the night that his visions had shown him. He loved the nights with warm feet and a happy dog on them.

INDIGO DREAMED OF A red dragon. He travelled alone and was on a quest. The quest was what Indigo was destined to resolve. He must find the dragon and help the dragon find the sword. The Blood Moon Sword that had been stolen from the red dragons.

He and the young red dragon were destined to save the world.

Indigo woke up and looked over at the old man.

He knew that he had just had his first vision. And it did not include the man who had cared for him all this time.

Indigo raised his nose into the air. The faint scent of smoke and burning trees came drifting in through the windows from outside.

Indigo rose up and went to the window. He looked out and saw the trees glowing with orange fire.

"Get up," Indigo bounced on the old man. "Get up now."

Nicolas sat up and looked at the wolf.

"The time has come," he said. "You must run. Go now."

"Not without you," Indigo said. "I won't leave you behind."

"You must," Nicolas said. "This night has been foreseen, and my time is at an end."

"Only if you let it," Indigo said. "Get up, now."

Nicolas jumped out of bed and pulled on his boots and a warm coat.

He led the wolf to the door and opened it for him.

"Go, now," Nicolas said. "I will be right behind you."

"Promise?" Indigo said.

Nicolas looked down at the wolf and smiled, "I promise. I just need to get a weapon."

He held the door for the wolf.

"Go now," Nicolas said. "Scout a clear path for our escape."

Indigo bolted out the door and through the front yard, accidentally stepping on the old man's herb garden as he went.

He tried to sidestep around it, but he was in too much of a rush to get away from the fire that was quickly encroaching onto the backside of the hut.

Indigo turned and waited for the old man to come outside.

When he did, Indigo shouted over the roar of the flames.

"This way," Indigo called out. "Come this way."

The old man had his staff and was heading around to the wrong side of the house.

"Wait," Indigo called out. "Come back."

He took a few steps back towards the hut, but then a giant creature came through the fire from the woods. It was a flaming demon that had its eyes fixed on Nicolas.

Indigo ran towards the old man, as Nicolas raised his staff and cast a spell to damage the demon creature.

Indigo could feel the heat of the flames as they licked from the treetops and burning embers rained down on the roof of their little hut.

Nicolas and the demon, engaged in battle, didn't notice Indigo's approach.

He ran towards the battle, and over to the old man's side.

"Run," Nicolas said to the dog. "Don't look into the creature's eyes, or he will be able to track you wherever you go. Run, now!"

"How can I help?" Indigo asked.

"You can help by running to safety!" Nicolas screamed at the dog.

He lifted his hand towards the wolf and gave him a soft zap of lightning that filled the air with a sharp crack and stung Indigo on the shoulder.

He yelped in pain and turned to run.

He ran as fast as his legs would carry him and into the woods on the other side of the forest, angling away from the town that he knew was to the northeast.

Indigo ran until he collapsed from exertion and he lay in the forest, fast asleep until the sunlight coming through the trees in dappled patches woke him up.

He retraced his steps through the forest and made his way back to the only place he had ever called home.

The tiny hut had burned completely to the ground and the herb garden had burned as well.

Indigo went out towards the trees where the demon creature had been battling the old man.

Laying in the charred remains of the edge of the forest, was Nicolas. His body was lifeless and severely burned. Indigo approached him and hoped that he wasn't dead.

Indigo sniffed him, searching for any hope of life, and nudged the man's shoulder with a front paw.

"Please, wake up," Indigo said. "I can't do this without you."

The spirit of the old man appeared in the woods and walked towards the wolf. His blue luminescence glowing, even in the daylight.

"Indigo," he said. "You must go now."

"Come with me," Indigo begged.

"I cannot," Nicolas said. "For I have other places I need to be."

"I can't do this without your help," Indigo said. "I don't know what to do."

"Follow your visions," Nicolas said. "Find the red dragon. I will be with you when you need me most. But until then, I must continue to battle the demon creature until you are far away from here."

"He's not dead?" Indigo asked.

"Far from it," Nicolas said. "It will come for you and it can only be killed with the Blood Moon Sword."

"That's what the dragon is looking for?" Indigo asked.

Nicolas nodded.

"Go, follow your destiny, find the sword, and then avenge me," Nicolas said.

"How?" Indigo said. "I have no way to use a sword."

"You will find a way," Nicolas said. "Now go. Find your dragon. Leave here and don't look back."

Indigo watched as Nicolas faded away into the trees.

The wolf turned back towards the unburned forest and ran.

More books by Judy Lunsford:
Gamers
Schemers
Fire Lily
Bezbell
Kirog
Fire Lily Omnibus
Moonlight Magic
Moonlight Melody
The Red Dart
Shadow Mountain
The Portal Wars
The Grimoires
For YA:
Life Unscripted
The Secret Gondal Society
Short Stories:
The Dark of Night
Fae Reign
Fairy Short Stories
Fairy Tales & Nightmares
Fantasy Faire
First Stories
Magic from the Dark
Story Hoard
Story Hoard 2
The Wild Hunt

Thank you for reading.
If you enjoyed this book, you can find more stories at
JudyLunsford.com
or your favorite online retailer.

Don't miss out!

Visit the website below and you can sign up to receive emails whenever Judy Lunsford publishes a new book. There's no charge and no obligation.

https://books2read.com/r/B-A-LRKI-OOFWB

BOOKS 2 READ

Connecting independent readers to independent writers.

Also by Judy Lunsford

Bird Lady
The Bird Lady: 10th Anniversary Special Edition
Seeds of Today: The Bird Lady Wedding
The Bird Lady Complete Collection

Crystal Tower
Rumtuskin of the Emberdiggers
Seeking Garille
The Indigo-Eyed Pup
Crystal Shards: Short Stories from the Crystal Tower

Fahlstrom's Adventures
Reality Fails
The Portal Wars
Fahlstrom's Library
The Grimoires
Shade
Family

Letters from Alexia
Letters from Alexia, Volume #1, Sally and the Buccaneers
Letters from Alexia, Volume 2, Sally and the Marauders

Moon Songs
Moonlight Magic
Moonlight Melody
Blade's Yard
The Other Side of the Fence

Story Hoard
Story Hoard
Story Hoard 2

The Wild Hunt
The Wild Hunt
Aeris Awakens
Aeris Redeemed
Priscilla Reigns

Trunk of Alexia
Sally and the Buccaneers
Sally and the Marauders
Sally and the Sorcerer

Standalone
The Autumn Fairy and Shadow Tail
Moon Songs
The Moon and The Moths
Airship Pilot Waffles
The Monster Bed
The Magic Pond
Life Unscripted
Trunk of Alexia
Fairy Short Stories
My Fairy Godmother Wears Biker Boots
The Rule of Three
Again Upon a Time
The Dollhouse
The Tank
The Dragon's Lair
Siren Bound
Luna's Adventure
Crafting Christmas
Fantasy Faire
The Red Dart
Alien Dreams

The Cat
Finding Ms. Blackwood
The Sea Journal
The Butterfly Boy
PlantMan662
Shadow Mountain
Pooka Deals
Beauty and the Three Evils
First Stories
H.A.A.
The Burning
The Secret Gondal Society
Monster Party
The Fairy Army
The Owl Rider
Halflife
The Fairy Godmother
Finding Mercury
Magic from the Dark
Marigold & Elfie
In the Light of the Full Moon
Touch
The Dark of Night
Number 37: A Short Story
Firebird Feathers
Check Mate
Visitors
The Reaper
The Journal
Fairy Tales & Nightmares: Short Story Collection
Junior Research

Charms
Ticked Tock
Voices
Fire Lily Omnibus
Marionette
The Gallery
Burn-Out
Circle in the Sky
The Rescue
Green Chalk
Lies from the Skies
Fae Reign
Truths: a short story
Stories for Kids: Short Story Collection
Monsters & Reapers & Ghosts, Oh My!
Dark Welcome - Short Story Collection

Watch for more at https://judylunsford.com.

About the Author

Born and raised in California, Judy now lives in Arizona with her husband and Giant Schnoodle. She spent several years as a clerk in a city library. Judy writes with dyslexia and a chronic illness & is a breast cancer survivor. She writes mostly fantasy, but delves into other genres as well. She has written books and short stories for all ages. You can find her books and short stories at your favorite online retailers.

Read more at https://judylunsford.com.

www.ingramcontent.com/pod-product-compliance
Lightning Source LLC
Chambersburg PA
CBHW051446150726
48000CB00005B/2268